JP/Loth, Sebastian

First published in the United States, Great Britain, Canada, Australia, and New Zealand in 2010
by North-South Books Inc., an imprint of NordSüd Verlag AG, CH–8005 Zürich, Switzerland.
Distributed in the United States by North-South Books Inc., New York 10001.

Library of Congress Cataloging-in-Publication Data is available.
ISBN: 978-0-7358-2300-6 (trade edition)
Printed in Belgium by Proost N.V. B 2300 Turnhout, November 2009.
1 3 5 7 9 · 10 8 6 4 2

www.northsouth.com

FSC
Mixed Sources
Product group from well-managed
forests and other controlled sources
Cert no. BV-COC-070303
www.fsc.org
© 1996 Forest Stewardship Council

Sebastian Loth

Remembering Crystal

NorthSouth
New York / London

Zelda was a lucky young goose.
Every day she got to see her friend Crystal.

Crystal had lived in the garden for many years.
She was growing old.

They were best friends.
They read books together.

They liked to swim together.

They took trips together.

And they talked about everything:
life . . .

their fears . . .

and their dreams.

But one day Crystal was not in the garden.

"Crystal was very old," the other geese tried to explain.
"She had a long and happy life.
Now it was time for her to die."

"No!" said Zelda.
"Where are you hiding, Crystal?"

But no one answered.

So Zelda went looking for Crystal.

She searched on the highest mountain . . .
(Crystal would like it up here, Zelda thought.)

and in the deepest ocean . . .
(Crystal loved the water.)

under the ground . . .

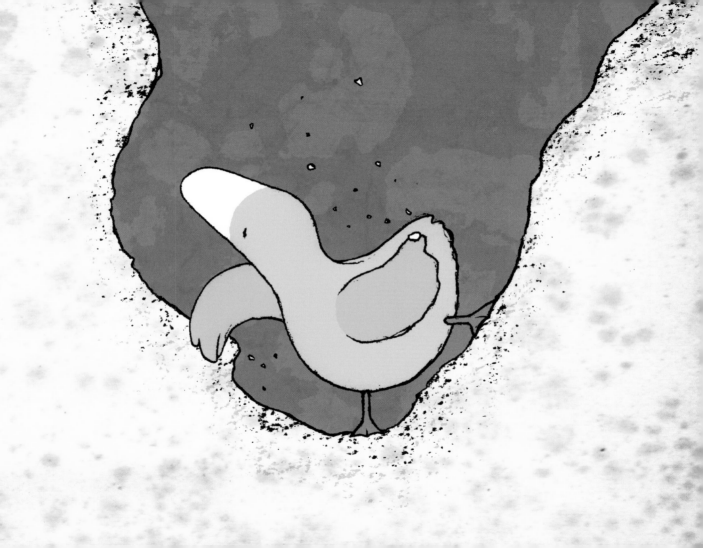

and high in the sky . . .

but she couldn't find her friend anywhere.

She remembered how Crystal
had taught her about music.

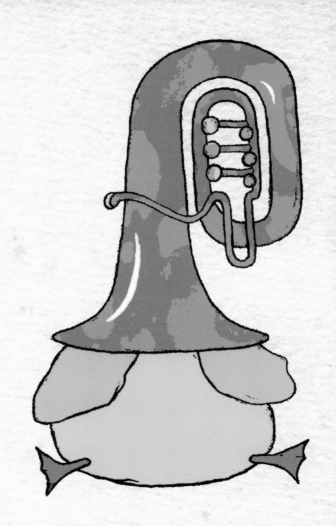

She remembered how Crystal
had taught her about art.

She remembered how Crystal
had taught her about the world.

Finally Zelda knew it was time to go home.

Zelda went back to Crystal's garden.

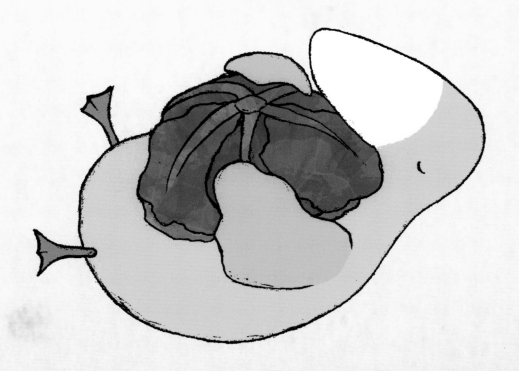

She felt very lonely and very sad.

That night Zelda curled up with her blankie.

She thought about Crystal
and all the good times they had shared.
She knew that Crystal was gone now.
But she knew something else too.

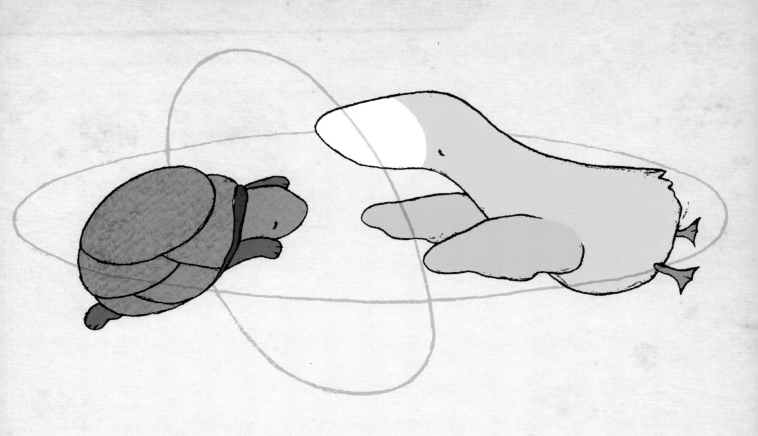

She knew that she would always remember Crystal,
and that Crystal would always be with her
wherever she went,
right there in her heart.